Accordionly

Abuelo and Opa Make Music

by Michael Genhart, PhD illustrated by Priscilla Burris

Magination Press ♪ Washington, DC ♪ American Psychological Association

The accordion is a funny-looking instrument. Is it a little piano? Some kind of harmonica?

My abuelo plays the accordion in a mariachi band.

When they play ranchera music,
he hoots and hollers louder than the rest.

It's a fiesta every time he sings.

And whenever we visit, my abuela
makes tamales and arroz.

My opa plays the accordion in a polka band.

When they play, he belts out a yodel that makes the windows shake.

He's the only person we know who yodels.

And whenever we visit, my oma's lebkuchen and hot chocolate make us feel right at home.

Abuelo and Opa always bring their accordions when they each visit me. Music and singing fills our home!

Sometimes I get up and move like a folklórico dancer…

other times I do the polka.

The first time my grandparents were all together,
one side of the table was *really* quiet.

My grandpas couldn't speak each other's language,
so they didn't say much to one another.

They said "please" and "thank you" a lot.

But not much else.

We spent the
day together.
In silence.

We exchanged glances,
but not words.

We listened to
the birds sing,
but we didn't
make a sound.

My parents noticed the silence, too,
and wondered if something was wrong.

"¿Qué pasa?" asked Mom.
Abuelo simply grumbled.

"Was ist los?" asked Dad.
Opa just scrunched his face.

The silence made me sad.

That's when
I had an idea.

I asked Abuelo to get his accordion.
Then I asked Opa to get his accordion.

Abuelo strapped on his accordion
and started to play "La Charreada."

Opa and I listened. And Opa watched Abuelo very carefully.

Opa began playing "The Yodel Polka."

Abuelo and I listened. And Abuelo watched Opa very carefully.

and singing together.

The blending of yodels and hollers broke the silence.

Music filled our house once again.

Watching Abuelo and Opa made my heart sing with happiness. With all my family together, in harmony. Accordionly.

My family is a mix of two cultures, and both sides of my family came to America at different times. My mother's grandparents, Frederico and Eulalia Sanchez, were both born in México. They came to California and had nine children. My grandmother, Agripina, was born right in the middle of all those kids. She met my grandfather, Secundino Castro, in California, where he was born—his parents had also been born in México. My maternal grandparents worked hard (he in construction and she in the fields and packing houses) and had two daughters in their small Southern California home. One of those daughters is my mother. She is a second generation Mexican American. She's in the photograph to the left, which was taken in Camarillo, California, in 1943. She is standing in the front right, her sister by her side, and her parents behind her.

My father's parents, Arnold and Mary (Ackermann) Genhart, came to America from Lucerne, Switzerland, where they were both born. My paternal grandfather worked as the head maître d' at the Biltmore Hotel while my grandmother worked as a seamstress and homemaker. They had two sons once they settled in Los Angeles. Their oldest son is my father, a first generation Swiss American. He's in the photograph on the right, taken in Los Angeles in 1942. He is pictured with his accordion, his brother, and his parents.

My parents met in Southern California, married young, and had seven children. This story was inspired by my childhood, family gatherings where these two different cultures came together, with my father right in the middle—playing the accordion.

—Michael

Working on this book has been such a joy, and so serendipitous: I am also Mexican American, my husband is of German and Scottish descent, and we also live in Southern California. And, believe it or not, my father also played the accordion! Illustrating this story brought back so many loving memories of him playing, just for our family, just for fun. My three children, much like the little boy in this story, enjoyed the beauty of being raised in multiple distinctive cultures within the same family. My parents are in the photo on the left; my in-laws are on the right.

—Priscilla

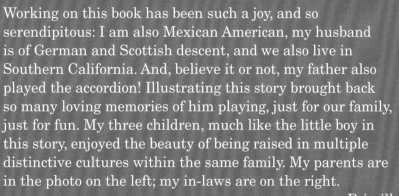

Magination Press
Books for Kids From the
American Psychological Association
maginationpress.org

Magination Press is a registered trademark of the American
Psychological Association. Order books at maginationpress
.org or call 1-800-374-2721.

Book design by Gwen Grafft

Printed by Sonic Media Solutions, Inc., Medford, NY

Cataloging-in-Publication data is on file at the
Library of Congress.

ISBN-13: 978-1-4338-3074-7

Manufactured in the United States of America
10 9 8 7 6 5 4 3 2 1

Soon they were playing along